LOOK OUT for Lightning!

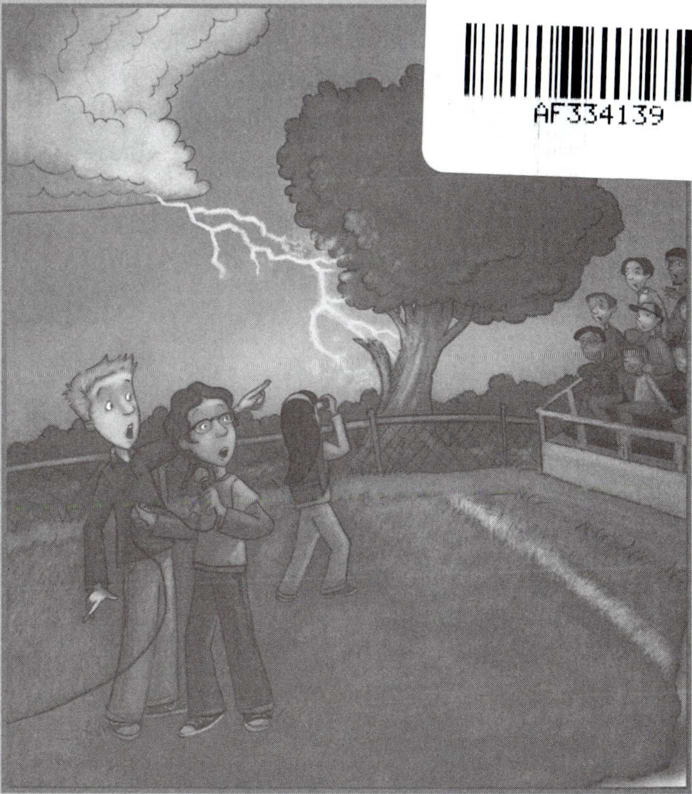

by Kathryn Lay   illustrated by Jason Wolff

magic Wagon

visit us at www.abdopublishing.com

To Michelle, my creative daughter. I love you— KL

Published by Magic Wagon, a division of the ABDO Group, 8000 West 78th Street, Edina, Minnesota 55439. Copyright © 2011 by Abdo Consulting Group, Inc. International copyrights reserved in all countries. All rights reserved. No part of this book may be reproduced in any form without written permission from the publisher.

Calico Chapter Books™ is a trademark and logo of Magic Wagon.

Printed in the United States of America, Melrose Park, Illinois.
032010
092010

Text by Kathryn Lay
Illustrations by Jason Wolff
Edited by Stephanie Hedlund and Rochelle Baltzer
Cover and interior design by Abbey Fitzgerald

Library of Congress Cataloging-in-Publication Data

Lay, Kathryn.
   Look out for lightning! / by Kathryn Lay ; illustrated by Jason Wolff.
   p. cm. -- (Wendy's weather warriors ; bk. 2)
   Includes bibliographical references and index.
   ISBN 978-1-60270-755-9 (alk. paper)
   1. Lightning--Juvenile literature. I. Wolff, Jason, ill. II. Title.
   QC966.5.L39 2010
   551.56'32--dc22

                              2009048831

CONTENTS

CHAPTER 1

"Today's meeting of Wendy's Weather Warriors is called to order."

Wendy Peters tapped the gavel on the card table in the center of the clubhouse.

"I'd like to order a pizza," Dennis Galloway said.

Wendy rolled her eyes. Dennis could be so weird. But she couldn't help but grin at her new friends. Dennis was nuts about weather experiments. He kept a notebook of experiments for every type of weather in his pocket. And Jessica Roberts was a photographer. She was nuts about weather photography most of all.

Maybe they should call themselves *Wendy's Weather Nuts.* No, they had decided on *Wendy's Weather Warriors* and Wendy loved it. They had come up with the name after they helped their school during a tornado a month earlier.

Jessica raised her hand.

"You don't have to raise your hand. We're not in school," Dennis said. He pulled out the black notebook from his pocket. "I want to show you both this cool new experiment I found. Got any balloons around here?"

Wendy shook her head. "No. Besides, I want you to see this amazing new video my dad bought." Wendy's father was a storm spotter and loved learning about weather as much as Wendy did. She thought they should make him an unofficial member of the club.

Jessica folded her arms. "Hey, I raised my hand to talk first. I have something I want to tell you about."

"Sorry," Wendy said. "Go ahead."

Jessica grabbed her backpack and pulled out a photo album. "I actually have two things to tell. First, here are the pictures from the tornado we had. Look, there's some of the cafetorium with part of the roof lifted off and all the mess around the neighborhood."

She held out the album to Wendy. "I thought we should keep it here at the clubhouse." Her tornado photograph had also been posted on the Circleville Elementary Web site.

"Great," Wendy said. She snapped her fingers. "We could have a shelf in the clubhouse called Weather Pictures by Jessica."

Jessica smiled at Wendy. "Thanks. My other thing is that Mrs. Stuard told me that I could be the official photographer for the big soccer match between Circleville and Diamond Elementary next Saturday."

Mrs. Stuard was the principal at Circleville Elementary. If she hadn't listened to Wendy and her friends about tornado safety, a lot of people might have been hurt when the tornado hit Circleville last month.

Dennis jumped up and bowed to Jessica. "Congratulations."

Jessica giggled.

From the corner of the clubhouse came a loud bark. Cumulus dropped the bone he was chewing on and jumped at Dennis. The Schnoodle, a cross between a schnauzer and a poodle, loved Wendy's friends.

"My brother is on the Circleville Cougars soccer team," Dennis said, scratching Cumulus behind his ears. "We're going to pound the Diamond Ducks into dust! Duck dust."

He jumped up and made an imaginary kick across the room. "And the Cougars score again!" he shouted.

Wendy cleared her throat. "Okay, enough about soccer. Like I was saying, my dad got this really neat video. It's all about lightning."

Jessica squealed.

Dennis put his hands over his ears. "Hey, what's with the supersonic squealing?"

"Sorry, but I'd love to get some lightning pictures," Jessica said. "I've got some cool lightning posters in my room."

Wendy nodded. She'd seen them. They were cool.

"Electrifying!" Dennis shouted. "Hey, wanna do some electricity experiments? All we need is a balloon and . . . oh wait, anyone got any spearmint breath mints?"

"Not right now, but I bet they would be great in class," Wendy said. "My dad said I could take the lightning video to school. I bet Mr. Andrews would let us show it during science."

Dennis and Jessica agreed it was a great idea.

Wendy said, "I wonder if Mrs. Stuard knows anything about lightning safety."

"I saw this video on the news once where this guy got zapped by lightning when he was mowing his lawn," Jessica said.

"Zapped when he was mowing?" Dennis asked. "Who mows their lawn in the middle of a thunderstorm?"

Wendy pulled a thick book off the shelf beside her ham radio. The title was *Wild & Wacky Weather Stories.*

"He probably wasn't mowing in a storm," Wendy said, opening the book.

"In here there's a bunch of stories about people getting struck by lightning on a clear day."

She read them stories about people getting hit by lightning while playing golf and swimming. One guy even got struck while watching television in his garage.

"I think we need to talk to Mrs. Stuard tomorrow at school," Wendy suggested. After all, if the Weather Warriors hadn't talked to their principal about tornado safety, everyone at Circleville Elementary might've blown away. She didn't want anyone at school to end up zapped by lightning.

CHAPTER 2

· Never Hide under a Giraffe ·

The next day at school, they were right in the middle of math when Austin Scott stood up in his chair. "We're going to smash 'em and grind 'em into the grass and wipe 'em out and . . ."

Mr. Andrews walked over to Austin and tapped him on the shoulder. "Are you planning an attack on long division?"

Austin shook his head. "No. The Ducks. In the big soccer play-offs Saturday. They'll be quacking big duck tears when we're done."

Mr. Andrews nodded. "Everyone hopes for a big win, but how about good sportsmanship, too?"

Austin sat down in his seat with a loud, "Quack!"

Mr. Andrews smiled at him. "Thank you. Now, as a treat, Mrs. Stuard has set up a little soccer demonstration with the Cougars after lunch today. I want everyone on their best behavior."

The room exploded with shouts. It didn't really matter whether they were watching the Cougars or watching someone eat a bug. Everyone was just happy to get out of lessons. Wendy was glad Mr. Andrews had already promised to let the class watch part of her dad's lightning video during science.

By the time Mr. Andrews told them to put their books away and pay attention to the video, Wendy's head was swimming with math problems and spelling words. But, she was always ready to learn more about lightning.

The video started with lightning flashes that leaped from cloud to cloud. Sometimes they connected from the clouds to the ground. Wendy knew those were the dangerous ones.

"Lightning is about 54,000 degrees Fahrenheit," the announcer on the video said. "That is six times hotter than the sun's surface."

Wendy's classmates gasped.

"That's why lightning is so dangerous," Wendy blurted out. She covered her mouth with her hand when Mr. Andrews looked at her. It was just so hard not to get excited about weather. And lightning was amazing. It could be so pretty and so dangerous at the same time.

When the video was done and the lights turned back on, Mr. Andrews walked to the back of the classroom. He took Bob the Boa out of his cage and walked around. Mr. Andrews liked to hold the class mascots while he talked. Wendy decided he did that to make sure the kids would pay attention.

"According to the video, is it okay to be outside when there's lightning?" Mr. Andrews asked.

"No!" everyone shouted.

"You could get zapped," Austin said, making a zapping noise.

"What about hiding under trees?" Mr. Andrews asked.

Katie Carter shook her head. "Trees are tall and lightning can hit tall things."

Mr. Andrews said, "That's right. You should squat like a baseball catcher if there's no indoor shelter nearby. Don't stand close to metal or water or tall objects."

"Like giraffes!" Christopher Richards shouted. "You shouldn't try to hide under a giraffe. We should all lie as flat as Bob. But never beside a giraffe."

"Or a telephone pole," Dennis said.

"Or Godzilla," Austin added.

Jessica giggled, but Wendy rolled her eyes. Austin was the silliest kid she knew.

CHAPTER 3

Cougar Mania

Wendy kicked at the leaves as she stood on the sidelines watching the Cougars run through practice drills. She liked soccer. It was fast moving and exciting. Her mother played soccer in college and once took Wendy to a professional soccer game. The players ran up and down the field. The ball moved like lightning between their feet.

"Go Brendon!" Dennis screamed. He jumped up and down as his brother got the ball from his teammate and ran toward the goal. Brendon kept the ball moving away from the Cougar who was pretending to be on the opposing team.

"We're going to win on Saturday," Wendy predicted. "I can feel it."

Kids were crowded around the field, cheering for their favorite players.

"Ouch!" Wendy shouted when Austin pretended to dribble an imaginary soccer ball and kicked her foot. "Watch it!"

Austin crossed his eyes at her. He spun around and said, "Watch out, I'm a tornado. Stop me, weather girl."

Wendy mumbled, "Weird." She moved down the crowd of kids until she could see Jessica. She waved at her friend, but Jessica was busy taking pictures of the goalie.

As she snapped the picture, the goalie stopped to pose and missed the ball that shot right into the goal. Brendon did a little bow for the audience.

"All right!" Dennis cheered for his brother. "Great sneak attack!"

The kids jumped up and down. The Cougars had a chance of winning the play-off game on Saturday, and Brendon was their star. Wendy could feel the excitement around her. It was electrifying.

She screamed, "Go Cougars!"

Wendy saw Mrs. Stuard standing beside Mr. Holmes, the PE teacher who coached the Cougars. Wendy pushed her way through the crowd until she was standing beside them.

"Mrs. Stuard?" Wendy said.

The principal smiled at Wendy. "Hello, Wendy. It looks like we're going to win the championship this weekend."

Wendy nodded. "You bet we are!" She cleared her throat. "Um, Mrs. Stuard, the Weather Warriors wanted to talk with you about lightning safety."

"Lightning?" Mrs. Stuard asked, looking at the sky. "It's a clear day, Wendy.

No weather warnings that I've heard about today."

Wendy said, "I know. But my dad got this really great video about lightning and I thought you should see it. I've made some notes about lightning safety and lightning facts. You see, it doesn't have to be a storm right here to—"

Mr. Holmes cupped his hands against his mouth and screamed, "Keep that ball moving!"

Mrs. Stuard shrugged at Wendy. "It's a little noisy right now. Why don't we talk about this later? I can see you and your friends next Monday before school."

Wendy sighed. She didn't like waiting on things. "I guess that would be okay. But, can I give you the notes I made?"

"Okay, give them to the school secretary and I'll look at them when I get a chance." She smiled at Wendy and turned to clap at another goal Brendon made.

Jessica snapped a picture of Wendy. "Show some excitement, Wendy. We're going to be the soccer champions in just a couple of days!"

Wendy crossed her eyes and stuck out her tongue for Jessica's next picture. She was excited about the game on Saturday, but she thought weather was exciting, too.

Everyone at school must think she didn't care about anything but weather. It wasn't true, but she couldn't help being interested.

Wendy decided it was time to call a special meeting of the Weather Warriors. She wanted to be prepared when they talked with Mrs. Stuard about lightning safety.

CHAPTER 4

Wendy sat in her clubhouse alone. Jessica was too busy looking over the pictures she'd taken at the Cougars' practice and Dennis was at a science fair with his dad. He'd entered two categories and hoped to win both.

Even Cumulus was busy. The dog had gone for a walk with Wendy's mom and her walking group.

Wendy wanted to talk to Dennis and Jessica about the lightning safety plan they were going to show Mrs. Stuard. But everyone was too busy with their own plans to come to the clubhouse.

"I don't care. I'll find something else to do, too," Wendy said.

Wendy stomped out of the clubhouse and into her room. She flopped on her bed then she picked up the song she'd been practicing for choir. She'd wanted to be a part of the choir ever since she'd heard them sing at the first school assembly. Now, she was in the third row between Tammy Stevens and Maria Rodriguez.

Wendy was supposed to practice every day. Mrs. Fenner, the music teacher, said they would sing at the celebration for the Circleville Cougars on Monday at the school assembly. It didn't matter if they won or lost the championship, the PTA had planned a special celebration.

They were going to sing two songs: "The Ants Go Marching" and a song written by Mrs. Fenner for the Cougars.

Wendy stood up, cleared her throat, and worked on memorizing the chorus of the new song.

"The Cougars are the team we love.

The Cougars will always rise above.

When passing the ball and making a goal,

Our team is always on a roll."

Wendy laughed. The song sounded more like a cheer than music. But Mrs. Fenner was a great choir director, even if she couldn't write perfect lyrics.

Something tapped against her bedroom door just as the phone rang downstairs. She kept singing as she opened the door and Cumulus ran in, jumping at her. He always knocked when he wanted to come inside.

"Wendy, phone!" her mother shouted.

Wendy set her music on her dresser, gave Cumulus a quick hug, and ran downstairs.

"Wendy, I did it! I won!" Dennis shouted in her ear.

"You won? That's great! Both experiments?" Wendy asked.

"No, but I got first place for my indoor rainbow experiment. I want to come over and show you and Jessica my trophy," Dennis said.

Wendy pouted, even though she knew he couldn't see her. "Jessica isn't here."

"Rats!" Dennis said. "Call her and tell her to meet at the clubhouse. I'll bring cookies to celebrate."

"Okay, meet us here as quick as you can." Wendy hung up the phone and dialed Jessica's number.

Just before the phone started ringing, the doorbell rang.

"I got it!" Wendy hung up the phone. Then she ran past her mom and opened the door. Something flashed in her eyes.

"Gotcha!" Jessica said. She stood on the porch, holding her camera.

"Hey, I was just calling you," Wendy said, blinking away the little dots from the flash.

Jessica giggled. "I'm not home."

"No kidding," Wendy said. "Dennis just called. He won first place with one of his experiments. He's on his way over to show us. He's bringing cookies."

"Yay for Dennis!" Jessica shouted. "Let's wait for him in the clubhouse."

Wendy took three bottles of apple juice out of the refrigerator. By the time Jessica finished posing Cumulus for pictures, Dennis burst into the clubhouse waving a tall golden trophy.

"See, here's where they'll engrave my name right below 'First Place'," Dennis said, pointing to the plaque on the base of the trophy.

"Cool," Wendy said.

Jessica pulled out her digital camera. "Hold up the trophy," she said, then took Dennis's picture.

They drank juice and ate cookies while Dennis told them about all the experiments he saw. He played tug-of-war with Cumulus until the dog yanked the toy away and ran off to play with his prize.

Then, Dennis told them about meeting the judges, "They were real college science professors. They looked at my experiment notebook and said I'd be a great weather scientist someday."

"Wow," Jessica whispered. "I'd like to meet some famous weather photographers and see what they say about my photos. I don't have a lot of weather pictures yet, but I didn't do too bad on the game pictures."

Wendy and Dennis looked through Jessica's photo album from the Cougars' practice.

"It's going to be a great game," Dennis said. "My brother will make so many goals, the other team will feel like they were standing still. My dad calls him Greased Lightning."

Wendy snapped her fingers. She grabbed a stack of papers beside her ham radio. "Speaking of lightning, I'm trying to convince Mrs. Stuard to read my information on lightning safety. But she's too busy with the soccer game right now."

Dennis shrugged. "Sure she is, we're going to be the champs!"

Jessica squealed when Cumulus dropped his favorite stuffed pig in her lap. She held it out and said, "Eew, dog slobber." She threw it across the room. Cumulus pounced on it and shook it until stuffing flew out of the toy.

"Is the soccer game more important than learning about safety?" Wendy asked.

Dennis nodded. "Right now it is."

Jessica pointed at her photo album. "I'm not into sports photography. But if I can get a good shot at the game, it might get in the *Circleville Times*."

Wendy knew it would be exciting for Jessica to get a photograph in the newspaper. But she wished her friends would help her plan their talk with Mrs. Stuard.

Wendy turned on her weather radio and listened to the forecast for the next few days. The robot-sounding voice announced that it would be clear and sunny on Saturday with a chance of rain in the counties east of them.

"I guess there's no danger for this weekend," she told the Warriors.

Dennis was telling Jessica about a scary movie he and his brother watched the night before. Even though the weather looked calm, Wendy still didn't like waiting to talk to Mrs. Stuard.

It wasn't going to be easy. Everyone was only interested in the soccer championship. The only lightning they were interested in seeing was a lightning-fast win over the Ducks.

CHAPTER 5

It was Wendy's turn to clean Sneakers's cage in Mr. Andrews's class. The hamster sniffed Wendy's hand when she reached for him.

"Hi, Sneakers. Ready to have your room cleaned?" Wendy asked.

The golden hamster's nose moved back and forth. His little black eyes stared at Wendy's thumb as if it were the most amazing thing he'd ever seen.

Wendy took all of the old wood out of the aquarium and washed Sneakers's water bottle, food bowl, and toys. Then, she wiped down the glass before replacing everything.

Everyone took turns taking care of the animals in Mr. Andrews's class. As a reward, the students caring for them got to eat lunch as a group with Mr. Andrews at his desk. Once a week, he brought sandwiches from home for the mascots' caretakers.

Wendy chewed her cheese and grape jelly sandwich.

"My dad says nothing is going to keep us from winning the game on Saturday," Dennis said as he finished washing his hands. Wendy was glad he had the job of cleaning Bob's aquarium. She didn't like snakes.

Austin bounced into his seat and stuffed half his sandwich into his mouth. "We'll smash 'em and trash 'em and bash 'em and gnash 'em and . . ."

Mr. Andrews cleared his throat. "Chew first, then talk."

"Yeah," Dennis said. "Say it, don't spray it, Austin."

"Besides," Joey Peterson said, "that's not being a good sport."

Wendy nodded. "I'm not a big soccer fan, but I think it's going to be an exciting game no matter who wins."

"We will!" Austin growled.

After lunch, Mr. Andrews told the class, "Tomorrow begins new units in each subject. We'll be talking about time measurement in math, explorers in social studies, and animal behavior in science. You'll each choose an animal behavior topic to do a project on."

Wendy's hand shot up. "Does that mean we aren't doing weather anymore?" she asked.

Mr. Andrews smiled at Wendy. "I know weather is a passion for some of you, but everyone needs a turn enjoying science topics. We'll do more on weather later."

Wendy nodded. She had hoped they could talk about the different types of clouds and she could bring Cumulus to school one day.

Animal behavior sounded like fun, too. Cumulus was an animal. And he behaved. Well, sometimes. When there were storms around or changes in the weather, he behaved differently.

Wendy snapped her fingers. She had an idea for a project where she could combine her love for animals and weather. Cumulus would be her visual aid.

She was going to be very busy working on this project, practicing for choir, and going to the game.

On Friday before the big game, Wendy tried again to meet with Mrs. Stuard to talk about lightning safety.

"I thought she said she'd talk to us on Monday," Dennis said.

"She did, but maybe she has time today anyway. I just thought we'd try," Wendy explained.

Wendy, Dennis, and Jessica waited in the school office while the secretary buzzed Mrs. Stuard.

Dennis pulled the small notebook full of weather experiment ideas from his back pocket. He tapped it and said, "There's a bunch of cool experiments in here on lightning. We just need a balloon or some mints ..."

Wendy nodded, "Yeah, you already told us about that. But make sure to tell Mrs. Stuard."

After a moment, the principal burst into the office.

"Martha, I need you to contact that reporter again who said he'll cover the game tomorrow. And call the food vendor and make sure he brings both corn dogs and hot dogs. And tell him not to forget the popcorn."

The secretary grabbed her phone. "Oh yes, these three said you told them you'd talk to them today."

Mrs. Stuard stared at Wendy a moment as if confused, then gave her a smile. "Yes, well, I'm sorry, but I am very busy today. I think I told you it might be best if we talked on Monday. I never knew almost being soccer champions was so much work."

Wendy pulled out a yellow folder and held it out to the principal. In jagged lightning-bolt letters Wendy had written the title, "Lightning Safety by Wendy's Weather Warriors."

Mrs. Stuard thumbed through the pages of neatly typed information.

"Goodness, that's a lot of stuff about lightning." She looked at Jessica. "Nice photographs, too."

Jessica blushed. "Well, I didn't actually take them. I looked them up online."

Dennis waved his notebook in Mrs. Stuard's face. "You want me to show you a great lightning experiment? Got any balloons? It's a hair-raising experience, I promise."

"Sounds like fun," Mrs. Stuard said. "But I really have to get to a meeting with the principal and coach from Diamond Elementary about tomorrow's game. I'll do my best to read through this sometime this weekend."

She tucked the folder under her arm and walked quickly out of the office.

Wendy didn't like waiting until Monday, but at least Mrs. Stuard listened to them. It was nice that she didn't treat them like little kids who didn't know anything.

"Come on!" Dennis shouted. "Last one to the bus brings the snacks to the club meeting tonight."

Wendy took off after him.

CHAPTER 6

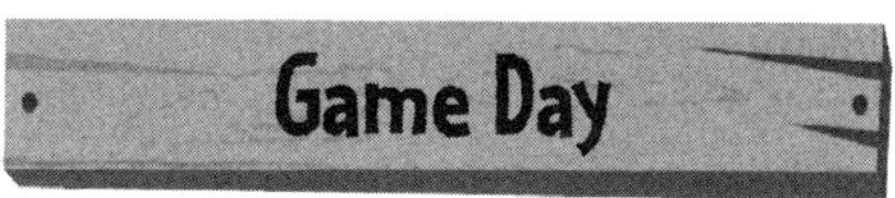

Wendy couldn't decide what to wear on the day of the big game. She wished she had a Cougars shirt. She grabbed a cream-colored shirt and a brown pullover from her closet. Cream and brown were weird school colors, but there weren't too many purple or blue cougars running around.

Wendy practiced the victory song for Monday's assembly while she got ready to go to the game. Mrs. Fenner said it was a victory song whether the Cougars won or not.

Cumulus wagged his fluffy tail and howled when Wendy hit a high note.

"Hey, I don't need a critic," Wendy said, hugging her dog. He licked her cheek and whimpered. Then he started pacing around her room, panting.

"What's wrong? You've been acting funny this morning," Wendy said.

She looked out her bedroom window. Cumulus usually acted this way when there were storms close by. But the skies were clear. In the distance, she could see what looked like anvils of cumulonimbus clouds. But, the weather radio had forecasted rain for two counties over. They weren't supposed to get any rain that day in Circleville.

"A clear day for victory," her father had said.

Her parents were coming to the soccer game, too. Wendy knew that most of the parents would be at the game. It was going to be crowded.

"Come on," Wendy told Cumulus. "It's almost time to go."

He licked her hand and followed her out her bedroom door.

Wendy thought about Cumulus's behavior on the drive to the school. This was exactly what she wanted to write in her report on animal behavior. Mr. Andrews gave Wendy permission for her mother to bring Cumulus to class during her report.

"Wow," Wendy said when they turned the corner to the school. There were cars everywhere. The parking lot had a sign that said, "Lot Full." A policeman was directing cars into the field beside the school.

"I hope we can find seats," Wendy's father said. He grabbed three cushions from the car and a small cooler full of sodas and water.

Wendy spotted Dennis and his dad sitting in the bleachers. Dennis jumped up and waved his arms.

"Hey, looks like the Galloways saved us seats," Wendy said. She ran around the soccer field to the bleachers where the Circleville fans were sitting.

"Thanks for the seats," she said as she climbed up to the fifth row.

"We got some good ones, too," Dennis said. "We can see everything."

Wendy's parents settled down beside Dennis's dad.

"Brendon is psyched up to win," Dennis said. "Better get your eyes ready to move a lot. He's going to be making those goals fast."

Wendy looked around the field until she saw Jessica on the sidelines. She was standing between Mrs. Stuard and the reporter from the city newspaper.

"Jessica must be on cloud nine," Wendy said. She turned to Dennis. "Speaking of clouds, Cumulus was acting weird this morning. He was pacing, panting, and whining. It was just like he acted when that tornado weather was coming."

Dennis looked up. "There's not another tornado coming is there?" he asked. "I checked the weather this morning and the meteorologist on Channel 4 said we won't have rain today."

"Yeah, I think it'll be a dry day," Wendy said. "Maybe a little wind from that storm over in Buckman. It's close, but it shouldn't come here."

The teams ran onto the field. Just as the crowd began to shout, thunder rumbled in the distance.

CHAPTER 7

The Ducks had the ball and were dribbling it toward the Cougars' goal, passing it back and forth. Suddenly, a too hard kick sent the ball out of bounds. The Ducks' fans groaned.

Wendy could hear Austin quacking from two rows down.

The Cougars had the ball and passed it down the field toward the Ducks' goal. Wendy looked away when she heard more rumbles of thunder. There were no storm clouds over them.

Wendy pulled out her dad's binoculars and looked toward the west. There were a few dark clouds and she could see shafts of rain on the horizon. The clouds lit up with light as the storm got stronger. Then a jagged streak of lightning seemed to shoot toward the ground like it had been fired out of a cannon.

"I don't like the look of that lightning," Wendy shouted at Dennis over the noisy fans around them.

"It's too far away to worry about," Dennis shouted back. He jumped up and screamed as his brother got the ball from one of his teammates and dribbled it down the field to the Ducks' goal.

Before he could make the point, the ball was stolen by a Duck. The Duck zig-zagged back to the Cougars' goal.

The Ducks fans were on their feet, cheering for him to score. When he did, the Ducks were the ones screaming. They were now tied with the Cougars.

Wendy saw another flash of light in the distance. It looked like it was too far away for them to worry about rain.

Wendy closed her eyes and thought about the lightning video. What had it said about lightning, thunder, and distance?

She snapped her fingers. When the next flash of lightning came, she counted, "One Mississippi, two Mississippi . . ." When she heard the rumble of thunder, she stopped counting.

Four miles.

The lightning wasn't very far away and there was a couple hundred people sitting outdoors. They were all unprotected.

If it got any closer, everyone could be in danger.

CHAPTER 8

Wendy grabbed Dennis by the elbow. "Come on." She told her dad where she was going. Then, she excused herself as she wove her way down the bleachers through the students and parents.

"What's the big idea?" Dennis shouted. "I can't see the field from here."

Wendy pointed to the storm in the distance. "Remember that lightning video?"

"Yeah, so what?"

Wendy sighed. "Remember how you can tell how far away the storm is? And how far from a storm lightning can strike?"

Dennis's eyes widened. "Did you count out the thunder?"

Wendy nodded. "I counted twenty seconds. Divided by five that equals just four miles. Probably closer now."

"Too close. It's dangerous to be outside," Dennis said.

Wendy nodded. The next lightning strike could be somewhere nearby. It could even be on the soccer field.

Wendy pushed through the crowd of people standing on the sidelines. Dennis stayed close behind her. They wove in and out toward Mrs. Stuard. She was standing with Jessica and the newspaper reporter.

The crowd around them started yelling and applauding.

Dennis stood on tiptoe. "Hey, what did I miss? What happened?"

Wendy ignored him as she stepped out of the crowd. Mrs. Stuard was holding a soccer ball and smiling as Jessica took her picture.

Dennis pointed at the scoreboard. "Wow, 3–2, our lead."

Wendy hurried to the principal. "Um, Mrs. Stuard, I'm afraid you're going to have to call off the game."

Mrs. Stuard gasped. "Call off the game? I can't do that. Look at the crowd! And we're ahead. Why would I do that, Wendy?"

Another rumble of thunder sounded overhead. Wendy was silent a moment as she counted.

"Sixteen seconds," she said.

"Sixteen seconds?" Mrs. Stuard asked.

"The storm is about three miles away," Wendy explained.

Jessica had been snapping pictures of the game. She lowered her camera. "Three miles? Uh-oh."

Mrs. Stuard stared up at the sky. "Why 'uh-oh'? That storm isn't going to rain on us . . . at least not for a while."

"The lightning might get us though," Dennis said. He whirled around as a shout came from the spectators. "Aw, I missed another goal. Our point!"

"You don't have to be in a storm to get hit by lightning," Wendy said. "It's already close enough. We have to get everyone off the field. At least until the storm is over."

Jessica focused her camera on the clouds and clicked as more lightning flashed.

"Cancelling this game is going to make everyone very angry," the principal said. She tugged at her curly hair and sighed. "We're so close to the end."

With a small smile, she walked over to the Diamond Elementary principal and whispered in his ear. Then, she stepped up to the announcer's microphone.

"I'm sorry to interrupt the game," she announced, "but we may have a weather situation. It seems that there is lightning in the area. It's not safe for us to be outside, so we're going to postpone the game until the storm passes."

The soccer teams stared at the principal with their mouths open.

"What storm?" someone in the bleachers yelled. "It's not even raining. Keep playing!"

There were lots of shouts from the other parents. Both coaches were yelling at Mrs. Stuard. The soccer teams looked from the coaches to Mrs. Stuard.

"Play!" the Ducks' coach shouted.

The Ducks started passing the ball again. The Cougars joined the game.

Wendy could see there was going to be trouble trying to stop this game. How could she make them understand the danger they were in?

Wendy ran to the microphone. She opened her mouth to tell everyone that it only took seconds for lightning to strike the bleachers or the players. Suddenly, there was a flash, an explosion, and a scream.

CHAPTER 9

A Warrior Rescue

"**W**ow, lightning struck that tree!" Dennis yelled.

Wendy had only seen the lightning flash from the corner of her eye, but she could see the black streak along the side of the big oak tree behind the school fence. It looked like someone had just pulled off the bark with a giant potato peeler.

Mrs. Stuard grabbed the microphone. "The game is postponed. Everyone, leave the field and go inside the school until the storm passes."

Mr. Holmes was already leading the two soccer teams across the field. He unlocked the back door of the school.

People climbed down from the bleachers and walked away from the sidelines as more thunder rumbled.

Wendy looked at the sky, but there were still no cumulonimbus clouds over them and no rain. The lightning video had been right. You didn't have to be in the middle of a storm for lightning to be dangerous.

Wendy waved at her parents and Dennis's father as they followed the crowd into the school.

"Get inside, Wendy," her father said.

Wendy nodded. She turned to follow Dennis and Jessica. Then, she saw Austin and his parents hurrying toward the parking lot.

"Wait!" Wendy shouted.

"Come on," she said to Dennis and Jessica. They had to stop Austin's family from getting in their car. Sometimes

Austin could be weird, but Wendy didn't want him or his family to get hurt.

"Stop!" she shouted again as more thunder echoed.

But Austin's parents kept walking. Dennis ran past Wendy and Jessica. He stopped in front of Austin's parents.

"Mr. and Mrs. Scott, you have to get in the school until the lightning stops," Dennis said, gasping to catch his breath.

Mr. Scott's eyes widened. "We're going home, young man. Did you see what happened to that tree?"

"Kaboom!" Austin's little sister shouted.

Wendy stood in front of Mr. Scott as he turned toward the parking lot again. "That's why you have to come inside. Your car isn't a safe place."

"Well, it's safer than standing here," Austin's mother said.

Dennis nudged Austin. "Remember what it said in that video we watched?"

Austin folded his arms. "I didn't hear anything about cars."

"Because you were too busy folding paper airplanes," Jessica said.

Mr. Scott shook his finger in Wendy's face. "Listen, kids, you all can stay in the school with your families if you want, but we're leaving."

Suddenly the sky was filled with light. An explosion echoed and sparks flew as lightning slammed into a van in the middle of the school parking lot. Jessica screamed and everyone dropped to the ground as car alarms were set off.

"We've got to get inside," Wendy said.

Mr. Scott nodded. The color had drained from his face. Everyone jumped up and ran back across the soccer field. Mr. Scott grabbed Austin's sister in his

arms. Austin's mother pulled him by the hand.

Mr. Andrews held the door open as they ran inside the school.

"Did you see that?" Austin gasped.

Wendy nodded. She'd never been so close to a lightning strike. It was the biggest explosion she'd ever heard. And there were sparks coming out of the car. Real sparks!

Mr. Scott stared into Wendy's eyes. "That van was two rows ahead of our car. We could've been walking past it when the lightning hit." He put his daughter down and leaned against the wall. "Thank you. You may have saved our lives!"

CHAPTER 10

And the Champs Are . . .

Mrs. Stuard went to her office and brought her weather radio to the cafetorium, where everyone waited for the nearby storm to end.

Wendy stood in a group of kids who were talking about the tree that was first struck by lightning.

"It was awesome!" Joey Ward said.

"Awesome? It was horrible," Bailey Hansen cried. "That poor tree."

Jessica showed them photos from her digital camera. "It could've been poor us. That lightning was close."

"Too close," Wendy added.

The cafetorium was crowded and stuffy. Wendy saw that both soccer teams were sitting together and laughing.

"Can I have your attention?"

Mrs. Stuard climbed to the stage and shouted, "Sorry, our microphone isn't working in here, but the weather reports say the storms to the west of us are over and there's nothing else nearby. We'll resume the soccer match in twenty minutes."

The cafetorium echoed with shouts and applause. The two coaches blew whistles and both teams scrambled to get to them.

"Whew, glad that's over," Wendy's father said.

Wendy nodded as she and Dennis followed their parents back to the bleachers.

Before long, the Cougars and the Ducks were moving the ball again. They were passing, stealing, running, and kicking. Brendon made another goal for Circleville, but missed a pass and caused Diamond Elementary to get another point.

When the buzzer sounded, the score was 5–3.

"We won!" Dennis shouted. He high-fived his dad, Wendy's parents, and anyone else who was standing nearby.

Jessica ran across the field. "Look," she said, holding out her camera. Wendy and Dennis watched the tiny screen as Jessica sped past lots of pictures of the game and the players. She stopped at a photo of the oak tree with the black strip where the lightning hit.

"Great picture," Wendy said.

Jessica smiled as big as the Cheshire cat in *Alice in Wonderland*. "Yeah, but that's not what I wanted you to see." She pressed the button a few more times. "Here, look at this."

Wendy gasped. The screen showed a streak of lightning shooting into a van, sparks flying like fireworks.

Wendy didn't know what to say. It was amazing.

The *Circleville Times* thought so, too. Jessica's photograph was on the front page on Monday morning. Wendy's dad held the paper up at the breakfast table.

Wendy couldn't wait for school. It was a big day! She was going to congratulate her best friend, give her report on animal behavior, and sing in the Cougars' celebration program.

Wendy's mother slipped into Mr. Andrews's class just as they were beginning their science reports. When it was Wendy's turn, she led Cumulus to the front of the room. He looked as if he were smiling at the class.

"Sometimes animals act differently when there is a big storm coming or a change in the weather," Wendy said. "For example, birds fly high in the sky when there is clear weather. Cows lie down, usually close together, before a thunderstorm. You might see turtles in the road a few days before it rains because they are looking for higher ground. And sometimes frogs are called 'living barometers' because they croak more when they feel the air pressure drop."

She caught her breath. She had memorized every word.

"Croak, croak!" Austin shouted. He hopped off his chair.

Cumulus whimpered. Wendy knew he wanted to play with all the kids. "The reason I brought Cumulus to show with my report is because he's the perfect weather dog for a weather nut like me. When there is a big storm coming, he starts to pace and whine."

She hugged Cumulus. Everyone applauded. When Cumulus barked, they applauded more.

Before the assembly, Mrs. Stuard pulled Wendy aside. She held out a small, red machine in her palm. "It's a lightning detector," she said.

Wendy nodded. "I saw one of these at a storm chaser meeting I went to with my dad. It's better than counting seconds."

"I'm going to keep it in my office, along with my weather radio," Mrs. Stuard said. "Thank you for making me listen to you and the Weather Warriors. If it hadn't been for you, we could have had a lot of injuries."

Wendy smiled. "You're welcome! Weather can be really dangerous. I'm happy we got to you in time to help!"

When it was time, Wendy followed the choir onto the stage. As she sang, she noticed Jessica pointing her camera at her. Wendy giggled just as Jessica snapped the picture. Jessica wore a T-shirt with the words, "I'm Loony about Lightning!"

Dennis waved from the side of the stage and pointed to his T-shirt. It was the same.

Wendy sang louder. She was glad her friends were loony. And she hoped they had a T-shirt for her to wear!

First Place

⚡ Lightning kills about 100 Americans each year, so it is important to learn about lightning safety!

⚡ During a storm, count the number of seconds between when you see lightning and when you hear thunder. Divide that by five and it will tell you how many miles away the storm is. For example, if you hear thunder before you can count to 15, the storm is just three miles (5 km) or less from you.

⚡ Lightning can travel as far as ten miles (16 km) from a storm.

⚡ If you're not close to shelter during a storm, stay away from:

- tall trees or poles;
- open areas, such as fields;
- bodies of water, such as lakes;
- metal objects, such as fences, sports equipment, or bikes.

- A lightning flash is no more than one inch (2.5 cm) wide.

- The temperature of a lightning flash is 15,000 to 60,000 degrees Fahrenheit (8,316 to 33,316°C). That's hotter than the surface of the sun!

- A stroke of lightning moves about 62,000 miles per second (100,000 km/s)—one-third the speed of light.

- Guinness World Records lists Roy Sullivan of Virginia as the human being struck by lightning the most times. He has been struck seven times. This is one record you don't want to beat!

MYTH: Lightning never strikes the same place twice.

FACT: Lightning often strikes the same place repeatedly, especially if it's a tall, pointy, isolated object. The Empire State Building is hit nearly 25 times a year!

MYTH: If you are trapped outside and lightning is about to strike, lie flat on the ground.

FACT: This advice is decades out of date. Better advice is to use the "lightning crouch." Crouch low to the ground with your hands over your ears to protect them from thunder. Then, put your feet together, heels touching. If lightning hits the ground, the electricity would go through the closest foot, to the heel, then transfer to the other heel and into the ground again.

Lightning Tips

What causes thunder?

Thunder is caused by lightning. When a lightning bolt travels from the cloud to the ground it opens up a little hole in the air. This hole is called a channel. Once the spark is gone, the air collapses back in and creates a sound wave that we hear as thunder. We see lightning before we hear thunder because light travels faster than sound!

How do you know if lightning is nearby?

If you see dark clouds, then lightning could be present, but the best thing you can do is to listen for thunder. If you hear thunder, then you need to go indoors or get in a car. Also, if your hair stands on end or your skin starts to tingle, lightning maybe about to strike.

DENNIS'S Favorite Experiments

A HAIR-RAISING ELECTRICAL EXPERIMENT

Stand in a circle and blow up your balloons. Have everyone rub a balloon against their hair. Look at your classmates or friends. Look in a mirror. It's a hair-raising experience!

Static electricity happens when you rub a balloon against your hair. That's because you are covering it with tiny negative charges. These charged hairs try to get away from, or repel, one another by standing up and away from the other hairs.

YOU NEED:

- Balloons
- Friends or classmates

MOUTH LIGHTNING

Go into a dark room or turn out the lights in a room where the windows are covered. Put a breath mint into your mouth. Keep your mouth open and chomp up the mint with your teeth. Look for sparks! You should see little, bluish flashes of light.

The sugar inside the candy releases little electrical charges into the air when you break them apart. The charges attract oppositely charged nitrogen in the air. Once they meet, they react with a tiny spark.

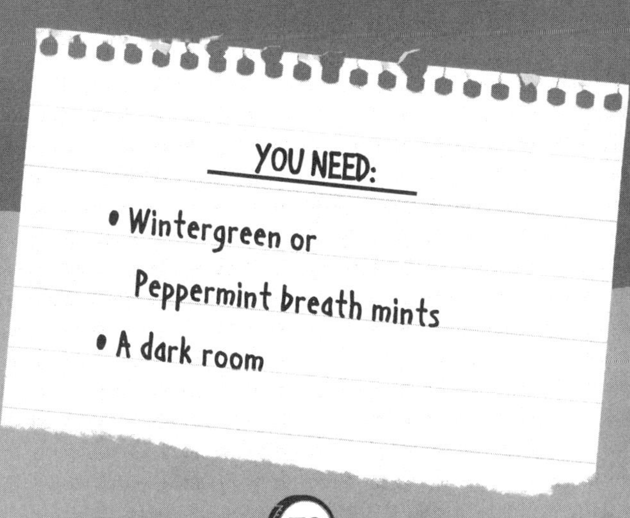

MAKE YOUR OWN LIGHTNING

Blow up the balloons. Now, make the room as dark as possible. Rub the balloons rapidly against the wool, ten times or more is best.

Move the balloons close to, but not against, a filing cabinet or a doorknob. Watch the sparks fly! A tiny spark should jump across the gap between the balloon and the metal.

YOU NEED:

- Balloons
- Wool clothing
- A metal surface, such as a doorknob